Quarantined

Writers Featured, Belinda Tam, Kian Isaac, Layla, Brey, David Supina, Tianna Schelstraete, John Christy Johnson, Kyrra Catherine, Josh Harnack, Samantha Skeich, Erin Pettifor, Ivan Top, Dr. Finn, Krissy Reid, Katherine Bessette, Toni Keller, Zoii Topia, Phillip Harrison, Rhys Westbury, Rebecca, Matt Niles, Woogie Luke Wohlgemuth, Landon Barrowman, Madeleine Landell, Phillip Harrison, Jennifer Wilson, Reinette Schabert, Samantha Skeich, Sara Ouellette, Peter Anto Johnson, Ryan Summers, Phillip Harrison, Yvette Mae D. Morfe, Tianna Schelstraete, Riley Witiw, Taylor Witiw, Lorna Radke, Natasha Corbett, Ryan Hook, Elliott Haviland, & Sabina Brouwer

First Printing: 2021

Typeset, Cover Design & Illustrations by Kayla Agustin

978-1-77369-631-7

Golden Meteorite Press
103 11919 82 St NW
Edmonton, AB T5B 2W3
www.goldenmeteoritepress.com

Quarantined

Written by
Sara Bruno
Brey Dawson
Rebecca Ryan
Austin Mardon

Designed by
Kayla Agustin

2021

My COVID Revelations & Learnings
A Poem by Belinda Tam

Over the past 17 months (18 by the time this is published)
since the pandemic started, many things have changed.

At the beginning, I remember the freeing feeling of being
able to go home and study for the rest of the semester but
also this feeling that this may go longer than expected.

As this feeling passed though, time went by very quickly.

Oil prices tanked – making me want to take car lessons … but couldn't.

Many students continued to pay rent for their sublets
because of contracts. I was part of this group.

The Australian Fire Season killing close to three million animals.
Many supported the cause of rebuilding, including myself.

Joe Biden won the 2020 Presidential Election.
Those who voted played a role in this.

The class of 2020 and 2021 graduated, some with jobs, some
without, some pursuing higher education, and some just taking
time off doing whatever it is that their heart desires.

These are a couple of events that have occurred in
the past 17 months, mostly outside my home.

These events and many others led people to panic too though.

Some examples include being laid off from jobs, panic buying
toilet paper, taking the money offered by governments,
and some individuals not only physically distancing
themselves but mentally closing themselves off.

I saw this happening in my personal life, on the

news, and talking about it in social media.

During this pandemic, many people are encountering
the same problems, but one group is reacting, while
others are choosing to respond differently.

These two things not only make up who we are as
people but are part of the communication process.

Realizing this made me change the way I communicate.

By learning about the importance of body language.

The difference between a video call, a phone call, and a text.

You see, me writing all of this and you reading it is part of a
larger process – me archiving a part of my life, you creating your
life, both using storytelling to do so, but in different ways.

By storytelling, I am communicating.

And by communicating, I am responding.

And by responding, I chose what I want to do
about the events I mentioned above.

You can do the same.

You can make an impact.

You can choose to respond differently instead of reacting.

As different parts of the world are starting to transition
back to in-person, some are forced or choose to
go back to their in-person workplaces.

Some get to choose what environment they get to
work in, whether it's from home or office.

Whatever the case, we are all human.

We should treat each other the way we want to be treated.

We should communicate, respond, make an
impact, and tell our own stories.

No matter the format.

I chose to do it here...

What will you choose?

Making History
A Poem by Kian Isaac

Tell your kids about how you were locked away,

like a princess in a tower is what you could say,

We're making history now, you see,

The quarantine in 2020 will live on in infamy.

Untitled
A Poem by Layla

I am tired of my heart breaking.

For as long as it beats it seems to break.

Careful, I keep reminding myself.

But a passionate and strong mind yields not only
powerful light but deeply defiant darkness.

This all too often, feels all too much,

for the fragile heart that bares it.

For it breaks and breaks and breaks.

And I sow and sow and sow,

And I am afraid for the day I run out of thread.

My heart has become so scarred and sown over
that it is hardened from the stitching.

And then they come.

Coping mechanisms in the form of big
beaming eyes and charming smiles

and there it is

Thump thump.

She lives. She breathes.

You must be the medicine.

I wish I could continue to believe this.

I wish you weren't my pain.

I wish you didn't have to always be a fucking lesson.

I wish I had someone that could be as patient with
me as I have to be with this process.

But I stand alone. Sowing my broken heart that continues to
bleed for a man who does not understand how to love me.

My feelings have never mattered to him.

Which is why they scream at me.

Tearing me apart from the inside out.

I feel the violent ignition of fire swelling like a hurricane in my throat.

Blistering heat. Throbbing pain. Suffocating.

I wish I could scream; but I am so weakened by your wrath
and so tired of this fight that all I can do is protect myself.

So, I find shelter from this moment and realize for the
millionth time that there is no reform to this broken man.

Your potential is not lost on me.

Your nature, however, is what I can never seem to recognize.

The pattern continues and so does the hemorrhaging.

But I will sow my broken and fragile heart until it is hard.

I refuse to give up on healing.

I believe that for as long as I keep this promise to
myself, the refusal to submit, that I will find a love that
feels better than the ones I have been shown.

Except unlike you, I will not have the expectation
that this love comes from anyone else.

To understand love, it must first come from oneself for oneself.

So, I will sit, and I will sow. And I will sow. and I will sow.

And I will make every scar count.

You are now fuel to the fire, the fire that is the pain, the pain that
motivates the love, the love I plan to share with as many as I can.

For you see, my greatest rebellion, the one thing you
cannot take away from me, because it is mine:

The ability to love more.

Gentle, whole and unconditional love is my revolution.

This is my legacy.

The mountain I will die on.

Creative ADD
A Poem by Brey

Today was a good day.

I started a dollhouse.

Why?

I don't know.

Today was a good day.

I am halfway done the dollhouse,

Floorboards down and furniture is built,

But did you see that watercolour video?

I want to paint like that.

Today was a good day.

I started painting.

I really like the different shades of blue.

Do you think that would look nice on a shirt?

I think I own fabric paints.

Today was a bad day.

I'm going to sleep.

Today was a good day.

I went thrifting and found some ceramics.

Time for a good old fashion DIY.

Why is there clothing at my crafting station?

Oh right! Fabric paints!

Today was supposed to be a good day.

I'm bored of fabric paints before I even start,

Maybe I'll go back to the dollhouse.

Or the painting…Or the ceramics…

Actually, maybe I'll just go to sleep.

March 2020 to July 2021
A Poem by David Supina

Here I am at the borders of the unbound and everlasting

Here in the wetlands of hell and the slow burn

Of purgatorial fire, I am enveloped in the lightless glow

Of yet another screen, and with deft precision

Constructed by months of a plight of sameness

Tell yet another that I am still all right.

Is it a word of a lie? Do I mean more

Than I hold steadfast to my life? No, but may I build

To the dizzying heights of living childless and without connection,

It is a time to ponder the deep crevices of memory,

Unpolished, unprocessed, unwept.

Like a lack of oxygen, there is a certain giddy

Pleasure in the solitude. What am I? Such questions rest

Until the days of slumber and quaking pass.

I rise, and fit myself into a familiar box to show my face

In a sea of black screens. I insist on presence

Mangled and perverse as it is, as if to say

I am, perhaps alone, still alive and here for you,

Even as we fade into perfectly proportioned grids,

Of names with no faces, for those who for all I know

May have died since we began this.

Somehow my grades have never been better.

Quarantine is less about the distance and more about the mind,

When every Dasein is danger,

When "to be there" is oblivion,

Only then does it make sense to risk life and limb for the Holy Sacrifice,

Which has never been more real, and never have I wanted,

So desperately to not see it on a screen.

I can feel the presence of my Lord in the offering,

Palpable, inimitable and ineffable,

But lost on a camera which leetches the light

But carries nothing of the essence.

The loss of my family as a dull ache.

They have built many a lonely wooden tower,

But the latest construction cannot support my weight.

How can I, papist that I be, join them anyway?

Their seriousness is either commendable or life by fear,

It seems the first but feels the second,

But is there a contradiction in being both?

I confess I never expect this to heal,

And I carried many wounds before this,

But the sting is not carried away by assurances,

That all necessary measures were taken.

I pray nightly for the end of this.

One wave, two wave, three wave,

And even as the eyes of the world slowly seem to reopen,

Is this but a breath before submerging into

The abyss yet again? I pray,

But why should God reckon my pitiful state,

As one who efficaciously can ask for rain?

I am no Elijah, I am no prophet,

I am nobody's father in any sense.

I don't believe in life without severity anymore.

May I never clutch kindness so tightly it dissolves,

And may I never treat with gentleness that which cries "justice!".

Surely there can be severe mercies, for have we not lived one?

The grace of God is good done both because, and in spite.

Another severe mercy and I shall wither away.

I shall remember this as the time when I learned to invoke the Blessed Mother.

I ask her still to grant peace again to this earth.

Untitled
A Poem by Tianna Schelstraete

how am i to make waves

when i am confined to a pond

Hemorrhage
A Poem by John Christy Johnson

What would you need to allow

a bleeding heart to heal?

You can stent it or seal it

But there's a limit with steel

We wear it on sleeves

And tug at its strings,

But the organ belongs

between thoracic wings

Sixty-five bpm,

What it does to sustain,

The lub-dub rhythm

In artery or in vain?

So don't allow vessels

To clot with clutter,

Regurgitate this:

Let no valve flutter

Quell the resentment

And quell the rage

So the ruptures may recede,

Like remains that age

The scars are proof of resilience

That trauma and terror could not silence

That our hearts survived the violence

And hold no grudge for vengeance

Untitled
A Poem By Kyrra Catherine

I can't get a grip at the situation at hand...No two meters at hand

We can't take a stand cause government forbid we band together

Nah they want you in crisis mode

Locked in, locked down, locked away

From anyone who might infect you while subtly injecting th projection

Of how you need them to control the uncontrollable

They want you hooked on their show

And we can't even say no cause they've taken our rights

Disguised as our knights in shining armour

Aren't you tired of being afraid? Aren't you tired of being saved? Aren't you tired of an invisible war?

You're tuned in to the T.V. where they feed you this story of COVID-19

But what happens if you step back into your own reality?

You're so close to the screen it's blinding you to the ripples unseen

We are creating a world where our kids are taught

Security is more important than affection

"Protection" is more important than connection

You know what they do to humans in prison? Isolation

Only now they've pumped you with fear and renamed it salvation

A life of many threads

There are times I think of my life and wish I knew where I was going

I have this idea that life is directional, that I should just aim and be on my way

But life is a tale of twists and turns

I imagine watching a spider weave and maneuver its body

Each movement adding layers and dimension

Does he move with the full picture in mind? Or does he simply trust the process?

Weaving this web of many threads

Life gives us all we need but how willing are we to patiently lay each thread

To let it all connect

To build this foundation for catching the bigger blessings

How willing are we to learn the intricacies of our own abilities

To move in such ways each thread builds upon the last

Expression is our weapon in a world that wants us weighted

And sometimes its so blatantly obvious I wanna fucking scream

They sell it like a suit of armour because you should be afraid

Just like that caught in their trap because now you think you need them

That's there play to get you to pay giving your power away to the fear they planted in your brain

Like a computer virus that keeps on popping up. And up. And up.

People wonder if they're living in a simulation blind to the assimilation through stimulation dulling away our creation

Expression is our weapon in a world that wants us weighted

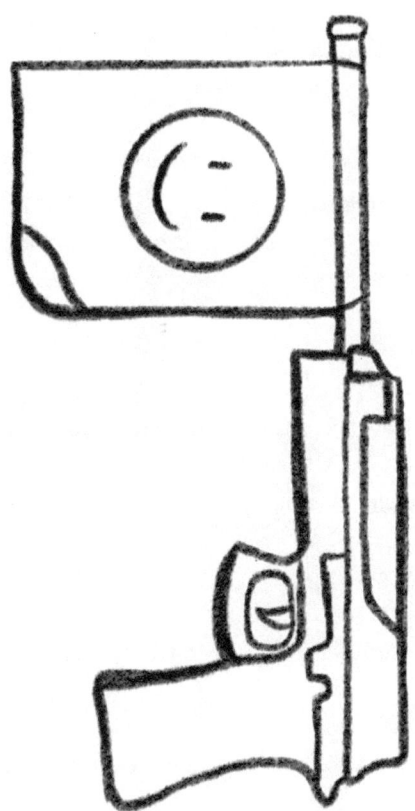

Surrounded.
A Poem by Layla

There are few places, people and spaces that roar louder than my inner-verse.

This makes my brand of silence unique.

My heart aches as it grieves a certain symphonic boom.

The energetic wave of the stage.

Performance.

This is where I come to feel silenced.

Flow.

I surrender to the amplitude.

This is where I feel safest.

I am viscerally present.

I can turn the noise off. Process holistically. Move freely.

It is the power of the collective that allows the release. I relinquish.

Suddenly, silence is possible.

It humbles me and simultaneously I have the space to feel alive. Connected.

This sacred space is not my escape. It is where I come to re-enter.

It is the deep dive that ensures an "escape" is no longer necessary.

A stimulation threshold.

You see, my heart is a constant storm of volume.

And until I am wielded by the power of the collective, I feel unable to submit.

It is not the inebriation or the validation that my soul is aching without.

It is serenity.

The stage is my stillness.

I accept that I am chaos.

And with the constant noise...

You see, it is my favourite place to be alone.

Surrounded.

Call of Duty
A Poem by Josh Harnack

A thousand respawns,

And we haven't won the war.

Maybe tomorrow,

So I die a little more.

Stimulated by fiction,

Stunned by reality.

I want to kill myself,

Bouncing Betty.

The Glass Castle +
A Poem By Samantha Skeich

i look up and see an endless sky,

but I've built my walls too high.

and after a year of closing myself off,

I now live in a glass castle.

people can burn, they've scorched me before;

"you are too fragile, you are too hard to love."

and after years of closing myself off,

I live in a glass castle, hurt no more.

my glass castle is fragile, but

rainbows dance across my skin,

as I allow new light to refract in.

you are warm, like a hopeful sun.

when it rains, i'll try not to hide;

i'll look up at the endless sky,

thankful for my glass castle

walls slightly less high

I'm smiling alongside those I've let inside.

in the end, this isn't a house of mirrors;

I cannot rely solely on my own affection.

i live in a glass castle,

I'm still working on my fear of rejection.

Untitled
A Poem by Erin Pettifor

I was an elegant misdemeanor gawking at the sky.

I lost my keys to my heart.

I lost patience.

I lost my virginity.

I found a blanket, comforting and wild, torn apart. I found a surprise.

I found an accurate Tarot Reading.

"I promise to love harder."

I turn off the lights in the bathroom. Epsom salts and lavender oil splash around me. I am in the womb.

Alone with the womb.

They are the gift in the storm, the clown who does not know.

They arrive when things have changed drastically, when all plans fall apart, my carefully planned schedule is disrupted. Everything I had always wanted at the tip of my fingers.

Life had other plans.

In my body it's at the tip of my nose, reaching outside of myself for answers.

In this, I realize, I habitually reach outside myself, palms open.

There weren't many answers available at the time. Only questions.

Answers began to reveal themselves as ancient rumblings in my gut.

I want to say hello, "I thought we'd never meet."

I thought I'd never have to breathe into the spaciousness of your unknowing lungs.

Pulling me wide apart, billowed at the hips, unlocking in the hollow of my throat, softening my sternum.

My irrational, unreasonable, completely emotional and illogical and entirely every single time accurate intuition told me through the rivers and droplets of sensation in my limbs that something was about to happen. For a while.

Answers began to reveal themselves as ancient rumblings in my gut.

I have an idea of what to do and say. My jaw locks up. Lips torn together.

We sit together. She watches me hold my breath. I watch her watch me hold my breath until I sigh out of peaceful resignation. She watches through my eyes, guiding my gaze. She tugs at my heart. More than a year later, she makes me laugh maniacally, sensing the presently enduring memory of holding more space for myself than I thought I was capable of.

Sit with uncertainty for a while and see what happens.

I can see myself in twenty years with laugh lines and a hard earned twinkle in my eyes.

Untitled
A Poem by Tianna Schelstraete

i miss you like cut flowers

miss the soil they sprouted from

In The Moment
A Poem by Rebecca

I want to,

So desperately say,

I got better.

All I can say is,

I'm still here.

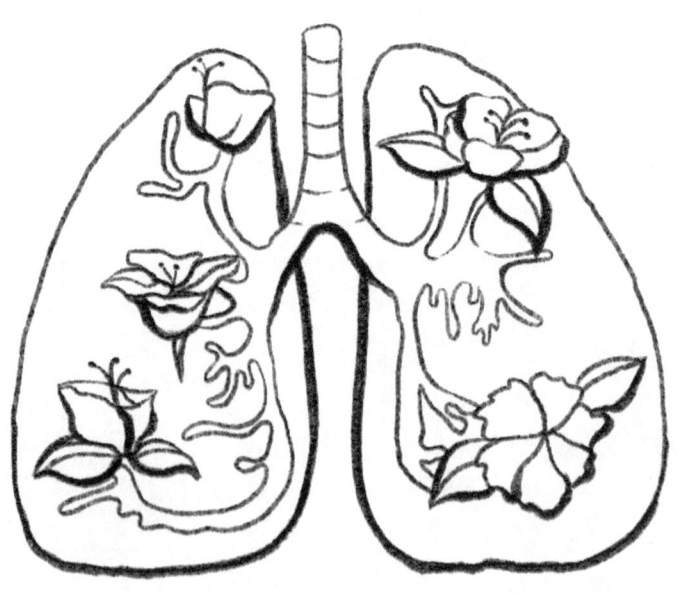

The Island Of The Deserted
A Poem by Ivan Top

Tried to live on an island dried and deserted

without voice or choice but to be introverted.

Drinking poisoned water and eating stinking fish;

trapped beyond the domain of even a vain wish.

Loose hope contained in the juice of a coconut.

Crying alone in a drying makeshift mud hut.

I had scrawled out an unread message that said "help"

that had been planned out primarily from sand and kelp

but there was just a fleeing chance of being saved.

I doubted if they cared if I shouted or waved.

Isolated from the sight of just one bright soul;

the shook pain of lonely existence took its toll.

Musing
A Poem by Dr. Finn

Calm breathing sounds

blue sky painted with clouds

Mastiff by my side

feeling quite purified

Untitled
A Poem by Krissy Reid +

I guess we're going this way, so I'll catch it up quick;

my feet are getting tired, and my shoulders feel like shit.

One month ago today he closed his eyes; away he slipped

I like to come prepared but I did not prepare for this.

I want to tell you everything,

the ugly and the cruel,

but there's never been a bigger chasm keeping me from you.

The distance yawns eternal

in a solemn kind of way...

Systematically, I vacillate from ownership to blame.

I should try to sleep but can't escape the irony,

twice in seven months I packed a bag to find sobriety.

It's not that it's been easy, but maybe that I've grown;

what doesn't kill you makes you sad

and then it leaves you on your own.

Then eventually it passes, just like everything else.

You realize the only constant in this life has been yourself.

I could ask for help and they could help me plant the seeds

but it's up to me to water them, my job to trim the weeds.

We're all a little greedy, little lazy, little stuck;

maybe now and then we find a way out of the rut.

Maybe someone makes it happen, or somebody has a hunch

that we're worse for wear, in disrepair (in layman's terms, we're fucked.)

We find ourselves forgetting how to build with our own hands;

instead we sit and wait for some direction, for a plan.

And when it doesn't happen it's so hard to want to fight,

when vertigo comes calling it's the best option in sight.

We're not born with tool belts or with helmets or with nets,

our schooling taught us nothing about death or deep regrets.

How does anybody learn to catch their breath

above the depths of the tumultuously unforgiving ocean in their heads?

Nobody's truly happy, everybody's getting high-

now we all wear masks, so no more half-assed, tired smiles.

Once I was a child with an imaginative mind

who made her mother proud by keeping colour in the lines.

Now I'm still a child with an imaginative mind

who's been confined to lines dividing us, "Keep back, six feet behind."

Be kind by staying in your home, save lives with isolation

we must protect the sick and old, the children of our nation.

Nobody wanted tickets for this ride to desperation;

our knuckles start to whiten as we grasp for transformation.

Poverty and war, inequality, disease

will be our passengers this evening, come along and take a seat.

We couldn't host a funeral, the signs above us read:

"No gatherings or services, be safe, stay home instead."

For all my troubles, I'm too privileged for statistics on TV

to have carved a real impact on my warped psychiatry.

We sat together watching the pandemic change the plot,

but we did it from the comfort of your couch while rebels fought

to save the lives of many, save those numbers on the screen...

Their lives were just statistics and their families,

fever dreams.

Is everybody sick like us?

Are we the only ones

that poison everything we love

and play the victims when we're done?

When I relay my stories, keep it vague so you relate;

we live in different worlds, but we both know that we're the same.

My novel's full of tragedy, addiction and abuse

written with a twisted humor and a couple of loose screws.

They say we choose our journey, but the journey chooses us

sometimes we stop to see the sights, reflect, maybe discuss.

We tend to think of turbulence as temporary gusts

in the momentary clarity between, we blindly trust.

This is when we'll take the pictures that we'll bring home to our friends

to convince ourselves and others that it's not all going to end.

Vacation's always over and the bars are always closed

so we hang our heads 'til Friday, back to autopilot drones.

We exist within a highlight reel, it's edited and staged

to keep us striving for those two weeks off, those benefits, that wage.

Our vision becomes tunnelled as we gaze towards the light

that we've been promised by the fairy tales that filled our heads at night:

"One true love will rescue you to keep you warm and safe

you'll face difficult lessons, but your happy end awaits."

I mean, unless we all complacently just scroll away our days

until the nothingness consumes us…

Fate showed up, but we were late.

You always claimed to welcome death like it was better than to breathe

but I watched you face your fate and felt you buckle at the knees.

I tried so hard to get you just to lift your head and see

you're not the only one who suffers, it's an everyman's disease.

A universal illness, treating symptoms, not the cause,

because to pinpoint any reason means to navigate them all.

No one has the time, we're busy chasing dragons

that were called into fruition in our own imaginations.

Then we wonder why our highlights aren't as shiny as the rest

like the rewards should come to us when we have no ambition left.

It's "2020 this, it must be 2020…" boo.

You think the world outside your door is what's to blame for what you do?

We used to hunt for nourishment, we used to read the skies

now we're scared inside the henhouse, too afraid to go outside.

We've got it made; we never have to leave our box,

protected by our apathy, our ignorance, our locks.

I was satisfied with silence 'til you taught me how to scream

you reminded me that fighting doesn't mean you have to bleed.

Like fighting for your sanity when it's about to break

and you want it to so badly 'cause you need the change of pace.

It feels like everything's dissolving and nobody's solved it yet;

it feels like every day it's harder just to crawl out of your bed.

You wake up with a sigh, look outside and you think

about how much you hate your boss and your reflection and your sink.

On the blinders go so you don't have to feel a thing

something blinds us all- maybe it's money, sex or drink.

For some of us it's easy, but for many costs our lives.

If the computers aren't the problem, maybe politics or pride?

When everything they've taught us becomes mythical, what's next?

Advertisers dangle carrots of the things we'll never get.

You, too, can drown in debt so you can cruise in that new model!

You, too, can drown in debt to let your brand new home sit hollow!

You, too, can drown in debt so you can follow that degree...

until the day of graduation, then we need the loan back please!

I'm angry you gave up, but I know more will follow suit;

if there's one thing 'bout rock bottom, way down here, it's only you.

The internet won't save you, no Prince Charming, don't pass go;

now's the time to either shift the blame, or time to grow.

If you didn't get a manual then fuck it, start from scratch.

If anyone has answers, they're to questions no one's asked.

...

Untitled
A Poem by Brey

Fuck.

My Own Midwife
A Poem by Katherine Bessette

Birth me from my small self to my Higher Self

birth me from my smallness to the truth

birth me from the finite to the infinite

birth me into you

cuz i am you

and you are me

and he is she

and we are they

and I know I can see myself in your eyes

so help me realize

the truth of the matter

that we are all part of each other

and my pain is your pain

and my beauty is your beauty

help me see myself as a reflection in your eyes

help me see myself in the beauty of your smile

help me know that I am not better

you are not better

that we are equal and we're stronger together

that we need each other

to get through this messy world

And the only way to it is through it

and there's no excuses

that will keep me safe anymore

there's no way to stay clean

while I'm living my dream

yeah its time to get dirty, time to explore

there is no greater truth than to be seen

in vulnerability

there is no better truth than to be seen

as a Queen

Great Mother, hold me tenderly

as I step out into this world, vulnerably

hold me gently, as bare my soul with sensitivity

diving into the Great Unknown

spread my wings rising from my cocoon

feel your heartbeat as I start to bloom*

help me be my own midwife

as I labour to live an authentic life

show me how to feel it all

to welcome and love the despicable

every day, every breath, every moment

every stressful thought

all this tension in my body

show me how to be the loving parent that i never had

in those moments of fear when i'm feeling insecure

show me how to be my own midwife

show me how to birth and realize

the beauty that is Me

For I know that I am God/Goddess

I am Spirit

I am Source of course

I am miracle manifest in this body

yes

help me to midwife the truth

help me to see through the veils

for I know that my small self pales in comparison

to the truth of the ultimate divinity

that is me

and I just want to embody

this knowing

in every breath

to feel deeply rooted

feel deeply anchored

deeply rooted, and deeply anchored

deeply rooted, and deeply anchored

in Myself

in my Greater Self

in my Greatest Self

help me be my own midwife

Rest Is Not A Waste
A Poem by Kian Isaac

I want to be better, I wish I could.

That's what we're supposed to be using all the "free time" for right?

Pick up a hobby, bake some bread, exercise.

Some of us are using this time for something deeper than that.

Tell me I'm not trying, I dare you.

Tell me how I'm not doing as much as I could.

The only thing to do now is rest.

When the world is on fire, and you're in the dark,

You Rest.

Terminal.
A Poem by Layla

There are toxicities in love that are beyond repair.

You and I, are by definition, a slow-release.

The type of illness that you so optimistically believe you can kick.

Dose by dose I sought to find the antidote.

Both of us are desperate for survival but mortal nonetheless.

Step, step, trip.

Fall, bruise, bleed.

Retry, heal, remission.

Re-step, step, trip.

Step, step, trip.

Step. Step. Trip.

Exasperated Acceptance.

Sometimes letting go is the only reprieve that can be given.

Surrender.

For there is no control in "terminal."

The irony being that Terminal is exactly what every last one of us is.

You and I are not a miracle.

Simply two human-beings, starring humanity in the face.

There is a you shaped hole in my heart.

But you see, this is where I plant my flowers.

Our toxicity is what has created the tenderness of my soil.

Through the rototilling of my mind, body and soul birthed my desperation for growth.

Addicted to the possibility of creating something significant out of all that is dark.

My silver lining.

My "You" shaped garden.

Where I go to plant my flowers.

With all the pain I feel, fear I posses, and uncertainty I face in love, there is one thing that I know for certain:

I would not have a garden if it were not for you.

And for this, if this alone, I am grateful.

Trippin'
A Poem by Toni Keller

I wish I could take us on a nice vacation perhaps Scotland or Japan

or a nice beach, with drinks in our hands.

What I can offer is a different kind of journey.

No matter where we're going

I'll be there and horny.

Untitled
A Poem by Tianna Schelstraete

as if creation was only for gods

you convinced me i was barren

that the lost cannot shape the contours of my hand

stomped a river with my feet

and grew flowers from places

you told me were desolate

The 3rd Date
A Poem by Layla

"We'll start with a foot rub"

He says with a smile

His offer is exact.

He knows my body so well... he does

He knows my fucking soul, he snarls to himself

Persuasion is his middle name.

Let me be her hero and soothe her with my cock.

The hero is absent here and he knows not of my soul. He should have never touched my body. I do see the tole I continue to pay in this misogynistic mess.

It stares me in the mirror every morning.

It was in that offer, to rub my feet, I understood how little he knew of my needs, my desire, my me.

But I'm a girl right, feminine by nature and a slit between my legs.

A body. A soul. A simple creature.

A foot rub.

His ego screams:

I know how to please you.

But it's presence is so large and deafening he forgets to actually ask, or listen as I say it.

You're so right, a foot rub. That will do.

I'm ticklish and hate being touched in this manner,

but what do my actual needs matter? Perceived needs and colloquialisms only here.

To speak truth is said to be overbearing.

I should just shut my fucking mouth and be grateful he offers. Says the clucking hens.

I mean, some men wouldn't even care enough to ask.

Believe it or not that is my preference. There is an honesty in the silence. An authenticity to the unwillingness.

We both know what this is, was and could be.

I am not so naive to fall for the ways in which you manipulate yourself.

But yes, a foot rub.

For this simple moment has a simple answer. And he knows it. I am to be taken as I have already lost my voice.

I don't even fully know myfuckingself, but you're right to be so sure of me.

After all, this is date three.

I Won't Be Home For Christmas
A Poem by Ivan Top

It hurts my heart we are apart this holiday

I despair that there cannot be another way.

I'd blame myself that we are not in the same home

but we're both mad and we both knew we had to roam.

We each stay in these far away countries for school

and now I only feel like a real lonely fool.

I know we can always plan to have a phone call

but I want to hear you near me; I want you all.

There's something special you bring in the face to face

now it feels like I sit and talk to empty space.

I try to pretend that my soul is full of cheer

trying to hide inside how much I need you here.

Zombie
A Poem by Brey

I'm bored.

How do I battle it?

I sleep.

I can't wake up, otherwise, I'm bored.

I dream of a vacation,

Swimming in the Ocean.

Going to a rock concert,

Sipping margs on the beach.

Instead, I'm bored.

I dream of an escape,

Some place far away from my bed.

A place where all my friends and family are,

A place that stimulates my brain and reanimates my soul.

Instead, I'm bored.

I stare at the ceiling.

Allowing unwanted thoughts to creep in.

All motivation has been lost,

Because why keep moving when everything is still?

So I sleep, because I'm bored.

crISIS +
A Poem by Zoii Topia

Isis: the Egyptian moon goddess whom, in mythology, was known as the goddess of life. Isis was most recognized for her great powers of healing, protection, and magic. At the onset of the pandemic, I sat at my altar, in meditation. The word crisis kept coming to me, and this poem (which is actually a rap) flowed through me. Later, as I worked through my own 'awakening' I found solace in the protection amulets of ancient Isis traditions, and therefore, renamed this poem from crisis, to crISIS.

Crisis happening!

Lungs malfunction

Threatening.

~aWAKEning~

Panicking

Or centering

Our own well being.

The streets have

NO

People.

I'm down on my knees,

Eyes to the steeple.

The old are the feeble.

This poem is my easel

Holding my heART

Through this fucked up ordeal-

Upheaval.

It's evil

Medieval

this pandemic crisis-

Calling on Isis!!!

This whole ordeal,

Worse than bronchitis.

We need get real.

We fucked up… surreal.

Creative licence?

Pray for

All patients,

We hope they can heal!

Patient.

Reliance.

Impatience.

Compliance.

Our trust in

Lord science.

We just want alliance,

With purpose filled

Guidance.

Too much time

Inside my mind!

I'm going crazy,

Hazy, lazy!

Too much daze

To phase me.

Praying:

"Help The Mother!

Stop Delaying!"

Breath fresh air,

No gasping,

Craving changes coming-

Time's a wasting.

People dying

Petrifying

Culture crying

Inside lying

Still with all my thoughts,

My mind a paradox

People dying

Petrifying

Culture crying

Inside lying

Still with all my thoughts,

My mind a paradox

Pandemic

Panic

Different

Dynamic

Ethic and Havoc

God

Academic

Natural

Genetic

Fake And Synthetic

Electromagnetic Forces Angelic

Shits Psychedelic

Psychic

I tell it

Truth be revealed

I buy it

I sell it

Crazy this world

Showing us

How we failed

Sit with

My feelings

Get real with my dealings

No damn way

I'm getting stuck here all day,

But there's no place to escape

So all day drinking cabernet.

First responders wear the cape,

Super heroes take their shape,

Overwhelmed and overworked,

But they do it every day.

People Dying

Petrifying

Culture Crying

Inside Lying

Still with all my thoughts,

My mind a paradox.

People Dying

Petrifying

Culture Crying

Inside Lying

Still with all my thoughts,

My mind a paradox.

How bout you?

Hey?

YOU

ok?

How bout you?

Hey?

Are

WE

Ok?

Catacomb
A Poem by Phillip Harrison

Darkened into twilight landing

Lowered into tombs descending

Dust in streaming lights departing

Quiet as a grave remaining

Tears from bowing eyelids leaking

Dirt to lowered coffins seeping

Rites and prayers, soft whisperings

And feet of the living, shifting

These are the graves, beloved resting

Here in sunlight, no one visiting

Family sparse, here were standing

Now all are together laying.

Into ages distant drifting

Long forgotten markers aging

Hear the black birds loudly crowing

Watch the grass above it growing

Biography of Phillip L. Harrison

Phillip is a Canadian poet. A Montreal native, he moved to the western prairies in the 1980s. Growing up in a large city like Montreal he explains, gave him a foundational perspective on culture and multiculturalism at a young age. His early interests and influences in writing led him to a persistent affinity for writing poetry. Phillip maintains that "... writing poetry releases the mind and its problems while sharing your poetry enables others to experience many of the poet's perspectives."

www.phillipharrison.com

Edmonton, Alberta

People In Their Places
A Poem By Rhys Westbury

Places to go,

People to know ----

This used to be it...

That used to be truth,

before our isolation hit.

Please, I have the proof,

I didn't imagine only...

Yet now I conjure...

Seeking my own respite

in avenues to wander,

it's falling into night....

Everything for all's unsure,

but one thing is clear

You can't come inside anymore ---- Though even over yonder, you're still near. I walk bit by bit,

Street lights are brightened,

Now every home is lit,

And I'm no longer frightened.

People are at home in through windows, A silhouetted couple start up
as I glance, Swaying into each other's shadows;

They own their dance.

Please, be faithful to my shadow, We once had a place for us

If you forget it in the 'morrow Rest assured, cradle it I must...

For they cannot banish

Our everloving touch ----

I won't let it vanish.

Maturing
A Poem by Rebecca

I hope that you do not waste the love I gave you

But instead

Use it to love her better than you were ever capable

Of loving me.

Another Quarantine
A Poem by Matt Niles

Captured in memories of quarantine past, my path laced with poison

And avoidance like a centipede. My shadow like a pitch black hole,

Life in a cemetery. Now it's here for all to behold

The fantasies reverse and envy turns hands, in my head I dance with glee

As you suffer in silence, my patience run dry, my sympathies quenched with money

The past repeats in a frozen Hell I thought would never come

I can't say hoped and can't say feared, I'm split between the two

I was the sickness, I was the cure, now I'm seeing you were not so pure

My shadow cast could have caught you, yours could kill with a snap

You know you're a walking, breathing disease, yet you hold nothing back

I knew I was a sickness, quarantined with less at stake

And anytime I extended a hand, I felt at heart a snake

I was a gun who hated his trigger, afraid he'd go off soon

Lost in a world machine gun black, led by butchers to slaughter

Now the butchers throw knives for fun, not with aim to kill, but aim at all

And the wrong slip of the knife could stab a lung of anyone close

Or any stranger on the street they speak to but doesn't know

The locks are broken, essential ethics tossed away

So you can enjoy what you call freedom, like a looter never caught

Leech to the world around you, no repercussions for what you do

Tables turn, true colours flash and a sea of red and black is cast

Tint of yellow for cowardice to all that can't take what they inflict

Live in the same reality, but erase you with a wish

Logic has kept me grounded, and empathetic to that struggle

Despite any petty emotions stocked, your humanity is also mine

I think the same part of me that wants to die, wants you to feel that pain as well

A bigger part of me wants to put out the fire, not add more flames to Hell

But how many hands can I extend when every time I feel them snap the joint

In myself and others, my bones have hardened, now I get the point

"My Challenge"
A Poem By Woogie Luke Wohlgemuth

Verse 1

I don't want this to be sad

I do want this to be true

just a few words I must say

if I can come clean with you

there are these things that I've been hiding

there are these secrets that I've kept

it's been going on for some time now

so many nights I have not slept

I'll do my best to keep the peace

try not to rock the boat

but when I go to say these words

they get stuck in my throat

I think the time is coming

I think you all should know

The Happy and the Sorrow

I hope you enjoy the show

Verse 2

For long I've craved to tell you

to let myself be known

fearing what you might say

or if you'll stay or go

To be fair it's no one's fault

yet responsibility mounts

It's not so much what happened

it's what you do that counts

the trauma causing me to hide

 it happened long ago

how ever did it come to this

only Heaven knows

I've been there and felt the pain

with Love I learned to heal

I teach you how if you'd like to know

so you know how it feels

Verse 3

In this challenge to be Me

to let myself be known

I'll bet I'm not the only one

Im sure Im not alone

how do you feel and why

do you know right from wrong

the meaning of your purpose

the words to your own song

We're the same but different

all going through our own

experience of the same things

tho we don't always let it show

what if we build our faith together

let's just see what we can do

If I believe in me

and you believe in you

My Challenge

Verse 4

Take the road less travelled

and walk the centre path

where everything is sacred

of love and art and math

light your lamp and let it Shine

sing your songs of praise

dance among the moon at night

and salute the sun by day

Magnets sparks and chemicals

with plasma blood and seed

 the currency of the kosmos

bio- magnetic Electricity

build a foundation for creation

 use body mind and soul

with actions thoughts emotions

to heal the challenge is the goal

Anathema
A Poem by Landon Barrowman

Oh to be hated

Disposed

Despised

Decommissioned

In Anathema

The white male in Anathema

The fighting masses in Anathema

Disease in Anathema

My neighbour's cough in Anathema

One thousand years black man in Anathema

Four thousand years woman in Anathema

Black woman are Anathema

Our world Anathema

There's no hope in Anathema

There lays your fathers dreams of tomorrow in Anathema

My hopes of peace , lost , dead , dying

Their atom bombs a Stone Age instrument

The virus is miscommunication.

Misinformation .

Everyone is told to bite the tail in Anathema

But the tail is their own

My worries and fears in Anathema

My apathy in Anathema

Oooooh can't say that in Anathema

Bart Simpson in Anathema

The Pope in Anathema

Walk down the street but step crack brake back in Anathema

Whitman, Ginsberg , Blake and Joyce in Anathema

Bebop and Rocksteady in Anathema

Can we live with Anathema

Cuz this is enough

We are all dying and a disease is making it quicker

Taking my loved ones

Can we put aside the differences

Or is that request anathema

The Banister
A Poem by Madeleine Landell

I run my hand over the banister

It's smooth with use

It's sparking with static

It's moving with me

I hold tight to the banister

The shopping is heavy

The people crush in together

I step to the left to stand

I step to the right to run

The banister drags ahead

Falling into oblivion below

Looping back to hold someone else

The banister feels different through the sleeve of my sweater

The suitcase is heavy

The building is empty

I step to the left anyway

The banister feels different bolted to the wall

It's static

I don't use it

I don't have anything to carry

Confronting your own solitude is a burdensome task. When days contort into weeks, and the same picture greets you upon wake and follows as your loneliness lulls you to sleep, what is there that stirs you to apathetically drudge in the same repetitive cycle evermore?

Sitting on a raft in an endless black ocean, the reflection of stars on it's surface deluding me, I wonder, upon which side do I really lay? I can't tell where I belong anymore, what is here and what is there. What comforts me more now? My seclusion? Or the visceral experience that comes with truly being alive?

I was used to cycles; I go to work, I run errands, I commute, I go to sleep.

Now, words are scattered across my screen, and I can't make out what was once so instinctive to me. I've forgotten how much I despised retail and conversing with customers. I can't fathom how I didn't fall asleep during my three-hour commutes. How did I keep up with the monotonous atmosphere that academia brought upon? Although I slowly see myself transitioning into normalcy, unlike before, I can't go to sleep anymore. Thoughts cloud my head and I wonder whether I'm the same person I was before.

Do I enjoy that work, those errands, my commuting? Who am I now? As my paranoia keeps me awake, I once again wonder, do I belong here anymore? On which side do I lay?

As the cycle remained stagnant, I've somehow managed to change.

Returning back to a world with cycles is daunting. All I want is solace, where nothing begins anew. There's a lingering tension that follows behind me as I attempt to integrate back into a routine once so familiar. Unease grows as critiques from the muffled tension tug at me and probe, "is this the life you were vying for so deeply? Is this what made your solitude so restless?"

As I look around, I now wonder, was it the cycles I missed or something more? Somehow it doesn't feel as though the person I am now is the same as who I was before. I don't understand what exactly I missed about work, errands, and commutes. I yearn for the melancholy that isolation brought, a cycle wherein I grew comfortable with having to avoid confronting how who I've become and what my motivations once were.

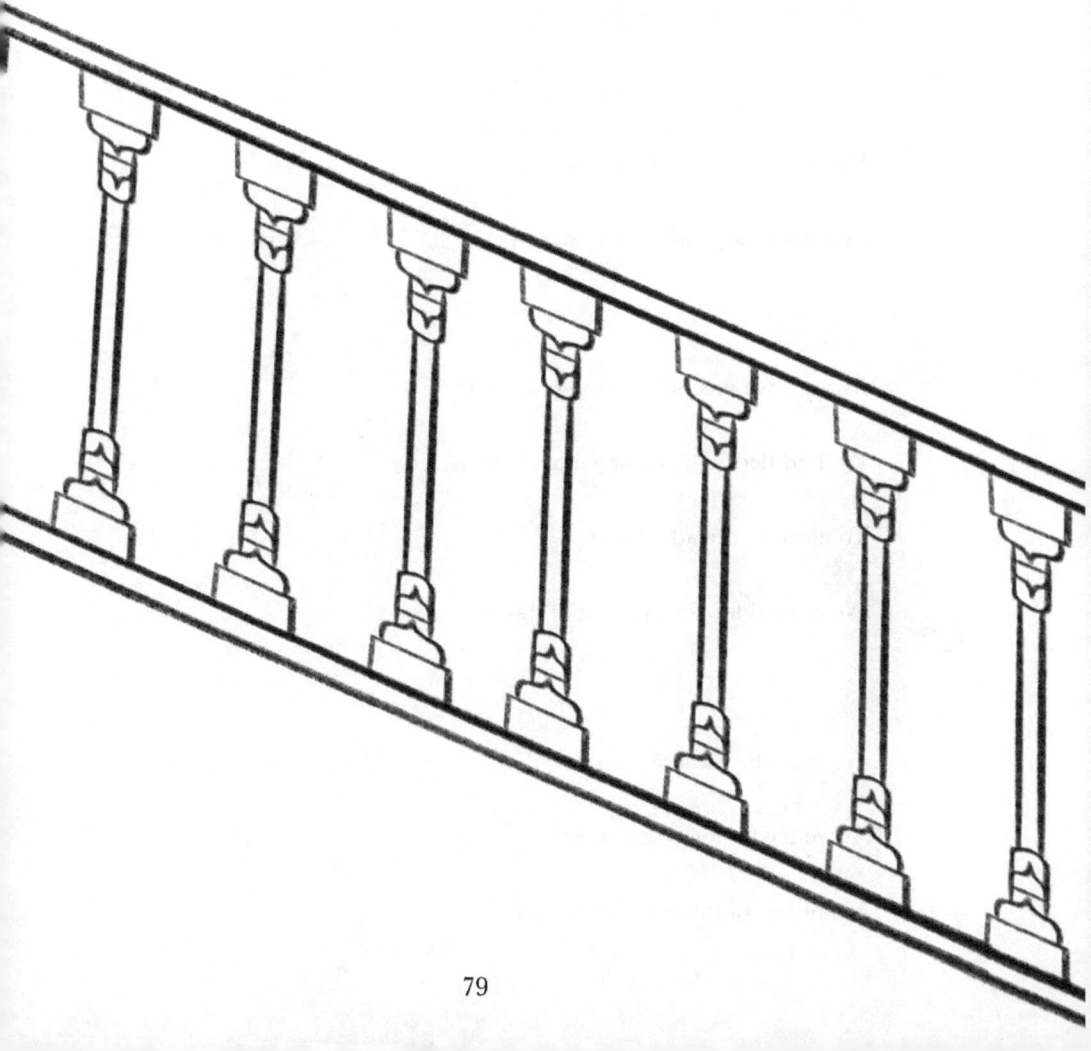

Dark Tunnel

A Poem by Phillip Harrison

Now the light, from the dark tunnel

Beckons, to each of our tired eyes

Sadness from parting and strangeness

Lost time, that has passed us all by

Heroes and saviors rejoice

As the long dark days have released

For now we can open the doors

Again we can walk in the streets

Many have passed, while we waited

We huddled in fear, they marched on

To eternity ahead, elated

We prayed for the coming of dawn

For now the darkness has yielded

As we try to normalize lives

Memories of those who have passed

Must still keep us, healthy and wise

They call from the borders of death

Whispering to each open ear

Don't let this passing pandemic

Quell all of your logical fears

For though the fever has broken

And each mortal soul takes a breath

Living, like this never happened

May summon the reaper of death.

What I've Found (look at me)
A Poem By Jennifer Wilson

Sometimes I'm a fuck up

And sometimes I'm a poet

But when someone like me breaks

Everyone knows it

Cuz I'm always showing my best face

Settin the pace and moving with grace

And it's only when it's too late

That people figure out that I'm coming in last place

Because I've made plenty of mistakes

Had moments that most people could never escape

And despite it all, I'll never break

It takes someone strong to admit when they are wrong

Too many times I've waited for someone too long

Tried to be strong

But now it's time to move on

These days I've learned how to unpack

to sit with my insecurities

And all of life's absurdities

Because everything I lack

Will never out-way the times

I've taken my power back

And with every fall

I've learned how to harness it all

The love

The shit

And every time I didn't know what to do with it

And I catch myself

Right before I hit

the ground

It's never been about what I've lost

It's about what I've kept

and what I've foun

91diVoC

A Poem by Reinette Schabert

Everything felt backwards
Sideways.
Upside down.

A wedding happened
Celebrated.
Bittersweet.

Locking ourselves inside
Separated.
Distanced.

A baby was born
Pictures.
Videos.

Staying at home
Working.
Trapped.

Thankful for the screen
Computers.
Cell phones.

A death occurred
No travelling.
No funeral.

Should have bought stock in
Zoom
Facetime.
Google meets.

Grieving tried to happen
No family visits.
No hugging.

Learned to stop planning
Quarantine.
Cancelling.

Connection through the screen
Headaches.
Frustration.

Reflections on my life
Society.
Relationship.

Exploring mental health
Exercise.
Religion.

Moving forwards stronger
Aware.
Understanding.

Vaccination research
One dose.
Two dose.

Waiting to burn all my masks
Wipes.
Sanitizer.

Three waves and more
Anxiety.
Bargaining.

Enjoying the small things
Safely socializing.
Exploring outside.

Thankful for friends
Community.
Alberta.

Being okay with
Being.
Backwards.

Solidarity
A poem by Josh Harnack

Trapped in a box, connected.

Alone, protected.

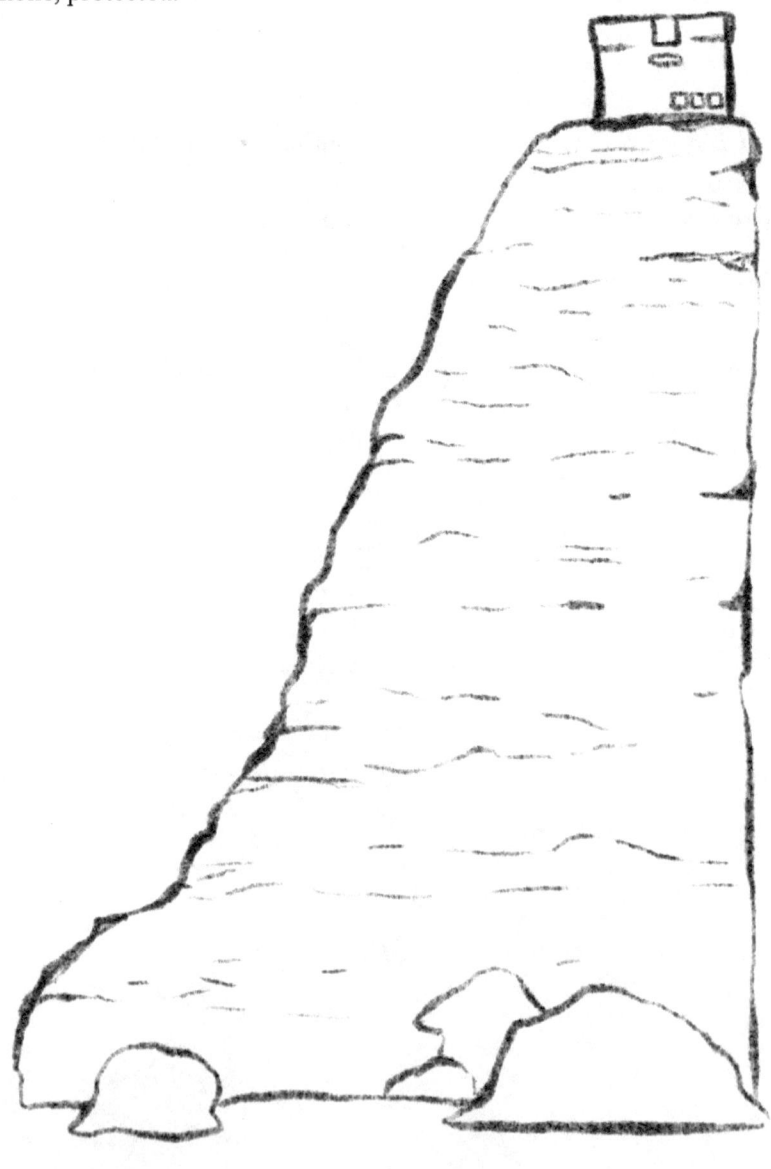

Sunset Darkness

A Poem by Samantha Skeich

Some are golden yellow,

like honey

dripping from a bee on a warm summer day.

the invitation to be consumed by such sweetness

is nearly irresistible.

Others are as delicate as a field of lavender,

tucked into a valley beneath grand mountains.

the invitation to lay my worries in a spread of tranquility

is nearly irresistible.

Few burn red, like a chilli pepper prickling my lips.

the invitation of the thrill, even for a moment's time

is nearly irresistible.

I am golden yellow, delicate lavender, and fiery red;

painted, consumed, by every being I've met.

my temporary breath of beauty

at the end of each bleak day

brings serenity and colour after a year of darkness.

Burden
A Poem by Layla

The lens we wear is the one we look through.

My chest feels heavy. A heaviness I haven't been able to escape. It's felt this way for so long that I often forget that it isn't who I am. My trauma. Heavy. A word I have identified with in so many shameful ways. Like a boot on my chest the panic sets in. Will I be cut off this time? Will the pain be condemning? I can feel everyone I love step back. The load I have been carrying has been too heavy, for too long. So, they tip toe around their inability to handle the weight with guilt and obligation. Heavy. It almost implies strength. But what of a heavy load and a fragile heart. The toxicity in me says dig deeper for strength. The well is dry. So I reach. And I fall. And I reach. And I fall. With nowhere left to lean, I turn to mechanisms. A boy, who will never follow my script. A smoke that will kill me without grace. A snort, that will make me sop with guilt. Food, that knows not of nourishment but is insentient. All burdens. Burdened. Burnt. Raw. Empty with no road or perhaps too many. Today I feel I need saving. But my saviour is tired and resting. She has left, because today she too can no longer handle the burden. So I will lie. Heavy. And maybe if I'm lucky. I'll suffocate myself to sleep with mechanisms. So all parts of me can rest.

I thought I wanted to live a life without you. But now I know that every step you take away from your abuser you wake up- and that is when we truly begin to burn. I guess forgiveness doesn't always look like the white light we wish it to. Today, it looks like an impossible burden.

So, for today, I'll burn.

Untitled
A Poem by Rebecca

Why do I feel so undeserving of the love I give others?

Phobias Survived
A Poem by Sara Ouellette

My worst fear has come alive

Sheer panic grips my mind

Symptom or not, I cannot breathe

My thoughts are quite unkind

You come to me for help

I must willingly comply

With a smile upon my face

I feel my sanity slowly die

Keep calm, have empathy

Play your daily role

Come home and crash again

You're losing bits of your soul

I trudge along each day

One foot in front of the other

But my biggest fear in this life

Is will I ever get to be a mother?

To have my own family

To hold dear to my heart

To get me through the day

Home is the best part

This illness is running rampant

Much like my thoughts

Dear universe please help

With all these twisted plots

Our world has been upturned

This is the new norm

I have faith that with love

We shall weather this storm

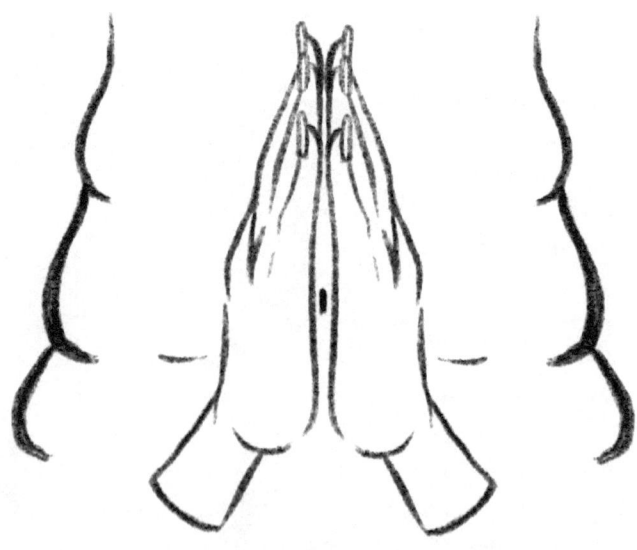

Asymptomatic

A Poem by Peter Anto Johnson

A thick fog contaminates my field of vision

Spreading a moment of blindness with every breath

Our masks drown the visage and its expression

That provokes uncertainty, which could parallel death

A persistent, painful parade of patient's passing

Pesters the pacing of a once rhythmic beating and rate

In a heart now overwhelmed by terror – no bypassing

The darkness of the plague worse than Middle Ages late

Emerging themes of variation, turmoil, and dread

Infect the pillars of what society's untouched mundane

Had once held – now out of hand and in one's head

Questions of life's value bringing a profession pain and disdain

Notwithstanding the variant times turbulence is the subject

Of shortage and scarcity from looming new strains

On a fragile system with a breaking capacity that will reject

Patients whose last breath leaves their membranes

Healing, though hurtful, is held as the only force

That we can supply amidst the despairing strife

To resuscitate ruin, wrecks, and recurring remorse

From impulsive distances carrying an invisible knife

Rage or resilience, killing or kindness, harshness or hope

Piercing society in every corner, these symptoms present

A new worldview heralding healers to widen their scope

As a herd heads to recovery and a few cough of dissent

Tracing waves and flattening curves in isolation

Superheroes bubble in wards at their brim

Where beneath double masks and perspiration

They clash to hinder a super villain's whim

Though asymptomatic, afflicting masses foremost

Is an illness – not that of a super-spreading virus

But rather one characterized by ego and mistrust

Evoking fear not confidence in those who inspire us

Untitled

A Poem by Tianna Schelstraete

sometimes i wonder if i would have withered

in my calyx, too fearful to bloom

flourishing is for the living

and my petals are lilac

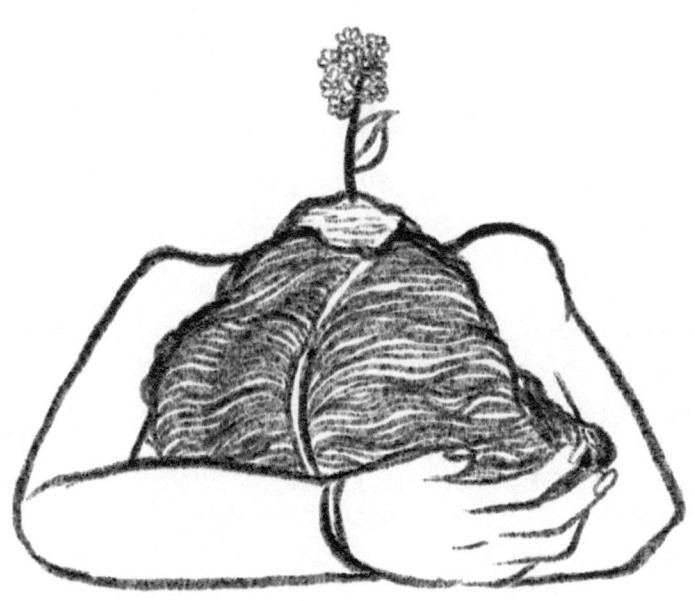

Serpent +
A Poem by Layla

I have been a serpent.

Although as I shed my skin,

Underneath the layer of protective scales laid a soft soul.

Someone simply looking for her cocoon.

Her safe place to grow.

But over time her softness turned callous.

Legs weary and heart foul.

Scaled over to survive, she slithered her way through.

Until she was capable,

of shedding that too.

You see, I have been a serpent.

But that was never really me.

Tethered in self-protection, never really being seen.

Simply a soft soul, with no safe place to grow.

You see, I have been a serpent.

But you do not blame a snake for needing to eat.

But looking back, the wreckage, it makes me feel weak.

You see, I have been a serpent.

Believe you me.

Untitled
A Poem by Toni Keller +

Hello World

Your arrival was long awaited

The coldest day of the year, you warmed our hearts with your presence
The isolation of motherhood enclosing

Just you and me, hiding from the cold

Brother is at school, Dad is off to work

Enjoying just me and you

Eat, sleep, play, repeat

Motherhood

Waves of crashing hormones

Tears with no cause, Why are we crying?

We cry together, neither understanding

The room is closing in, anxiety rising

Brother is at school, Dad is off to work

Learning just me and you

Eat, sleep, play, repeat

Crashing

Anxiety and fear closing in

Pandemic is rising

Isolated further from the world

Grandparents, Aunts, Uncles, Friends, familiar, turned strange

Brother sent home, Dad is off work

Learning how to stay

Eat, sleep, play, repeat

Exhaustion

You keep us awake, constantly tired

Feels like the world is burning, your smiles bring sunshine

Visitors not welcomed, longing for their presence

We need a break, nowhere to go

Brother sent home, Dad is off work

Pulling out of the fog, winter is gone

Eat, sleep, play, repeat

Release

The mother bear has arrived, I know her well

The fog is thinning, fear is lifting

Escape has been found, walks in the woods

Nature is healing, feeling the pain inside subside

Brother sent home, Dad is off work

Healing energies, the walls are lifting

Eat, sleep, play, repeat

Love

New found intimacy, truth in relationships Within these walls, we are our true selves, Surrounded by warmth, comfort, ease, routine Family and friendships are bound in stone

Brother is at school, Dad is at work

Just me and you and this new world

Eat, sleep, play, love, repeat

Eat, sleep, play, love, repeat

Emerge,
A Poem by Ryan Summers

From this cocoon of used mask refuse, hand sanitized recluse, 6 feet from touching you, can't see the ones that are loved unless they live with you, stasis.

It started at the end of a party, heard last week that there was a virus emerging across the world, people dieing, lungs collapsing, ER wards lapsing into over use and no rest for the nurses and Doctors.

I danced with her that night, one of the lights of my life, the blonde highlights of her golden bright sight captured in the shifting patterns of a night life dance rite.

I held my hands in the lasers, as she twisted my hips with the hypnotic and entrancing flavor of last year's lovers knowing. She smelled my shoulder as the rest of the dance floor kept flowing. Borrowing innocence free of this instance of a virus spreading in our air spaces.

Locked down,

Terrified, son not coming to the city, every lover unrequited despite the want I had for them and to be in their beds kissing away the frustration of failed relationships and moaning my goodbyes into the sighs of love's expression.

Internet,

Addiction to intimate space shared cut off and as the world wept the Irish men sung their despair, sports stopped, mother earth had a chance to breathe a drum beats length of healing herself and her hospitals stayed full.

Stay home!

I did, I stayed. I folded inside, showing the world my self care routines and running through snow filled fields of dreams I wished upon the stars and screamed my frustration at this circumstance. Wept for those who didn't get the chance to live through the pandemic.

And so, we emerge.

Evolved in some ways, barely survived some of the days, loose strands of hair from the overly tight braids, to stay, to breathe to play. And they will say one day we were brave and the depravity got to some, found themselves living at the end of a gun, a time to restructure some of the way the world is run. Labour shortages and power outages, as the median temperature rises and I'm here to say, that I'm proud of you today, I'm proud of me today and I'm proud of we today. We all have parts to play.

Emerge..

The Sentence
A Poem by Phillip Harrison

Behind this door of my own cell

I wait for death and watch it come

Our passing days, solitary hells

The world outside becomes undone

Visions before my eyes will pass

In solitude from others, wait

The sentence, from nature amassed

Now hangs above our heads delayed

All the wondrous things for granted

Our small pleasures misused, and spent

In forgotten seasons, planted

And lost times past, and pasts repent

We wander imprisoned here

Await news from beyond these walls

But days pass and the sentenced fears

Breaks minds and spirits, others fall

Falling, from cells to waiting rooms

Lost hopes, lost breath, in beds alone

The dead and dying, in nature's tomb

We're imprisoned in our own homes

Not A Constant Change

A Poem By Yvette Mae D. Morfe

It was one night of winter

Everything thy know change

Depart to an unfamiliar place

Feeling the coldness down to the soul

Every flake that touches thy skin

Melts in a single blink

Yet, you felt its coldness

But deeply saw its purity

Unexpectedly, the once pure white has been tainted

You feel trapped and cannot recover

Having locked up in the darkness

Is it a way of defending oneself from the outside?

Spring blooms without hesitation

Gathered courage setting foot outside

Only to witness giving the cold shoulder

The flowers gathered withered

Summer came but the darkness remains

The snow still lingers thy skin

Terrified of the vicious world

This thought of a burning question

Staring on thy hands in the gloom

You thought of nothing but desolation

But a sudden cold run down in your vision

Thy sight suddenly blurs in the empty room

Fall will end soon without notice

The feeling of uncontrollable endless misery

Wondering if this will ever end

Yet, standing firmly facing tomorrow

Day Something
A Poem by Brey

Day 1:
Let's get shit done.
Clean my room.
Organize my life.
Get this procrastination on the run.

Day 38:
Ain't this pause great?
Rediscovered hobbies.
Found the time.
The world can wait.

Day 123:
What even is vitamin D?
Been inside for weeks.
Seasonal affective.
Loneliness of the third degree.

Day 254:
I'm poor.
Fiscally? Check.
Mentally? Check.
Off to the liquor store.
Day Something:
Feeling less disgusting.
Accepted fate.
Learned gratitude.
Life will always have shortcomings.

Reap What You Sow +
A Poem by Rebecca

May your growth show

Within the seeds you sow

Full Acceptance +
A Poem by Layla

It's not about not loving them; it's about loving you more.

It's not that you are not loveable, it is that you deserve more love than some can give

and you better believe it's your responsibility to give it to yourself.

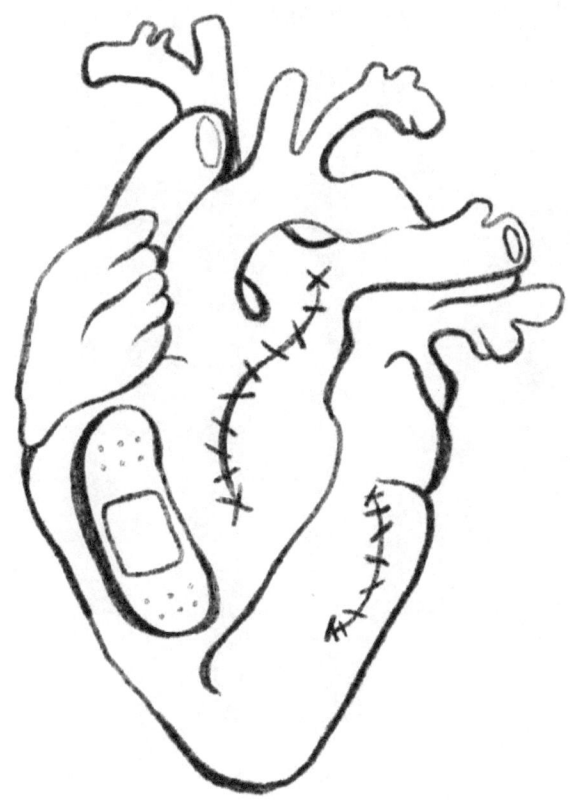

Untitled
A Poem by Tianna Schelstraete

i am not who you think i am

and possibly, you knew this

but my lack of inspiration

is not the absence of ignition.

it is the beginning of our end

of which you tried to prevent

by extinguishing me

Little Moleman
A Poem by Riley Witiw

Scurry, little moleman,

Go do little moleman things.

Like run in a wheel

Till the mechanism sings.

Take a sip from the bottle

Go poo in the chips.

Sleep in a burrow.

You're doing great, as long as you keep doing it like this.

Naughty little moleman

Neglecting little moleman things.

Too distracted by the cage,

And its little grates and springs.

You had all day to spin the wheel.

Before you sleep and drink and poo.

But now that time is over,

What are you going to do?

Hurry, little moleman

Rushing little moleman things.

Two days' worth of spinning?

Make those little feetsies swing!

You barely pulled it off.

Had to forgo your poo

To take a sip of water

And burrow deeply – phew!

… Only to get distracted by the cage and stay up late.

Fumes

A Poem by Taylor Witiw

Dear mothers,

sisters, aunties, moms' mothers—

space is the medicine they

say;

but fathers,

brothers, uncles, dads' fathers—

time passes and we grow aged,

caged.

Not fearful—

swayed, like the critics' earful—

still we barricade: "What of?"

Love.

Your faces

I see by inward traces.

Space cures. Time flies. Sleep, like fumes,

looms.

Together We Are
A Poem by Lorna Radke

So much of our lives together.

Heroes of stories untold--

emotions hinder and linger.

Yet to be unfold.

So much of our lives together.

Yet separate stories be told.

Our todays and tomorrows,

Will continue to unfold.

It wasn't short and ne'er so sweet.

Today not always tomorrow.

Ne'er-do-well as cold wind blows,

Then sunshine bestows our sorrow

The end of life may evolve.

yet stories be gladly shared.

All of us together we go--

Remembering we are spared

There are tomorrows

Not known to share.

Blessings the Spirit gave us,

applaud we are here and there.

Grief
A Poem by Kian Isaac

When grief and I kiss we use tongue.

It is messy and bruising,

Harder than I'd like.

I try to pull away, lighten it a little,

But grief isn't so easily persuaded.

It pierces through my chest like the bullet of a gun,

And sometimes I pull it closer because it's all I have

Because I'm empty

and anything feels better than that.

Within
A Poem by Rebecca

There will be moments where you will not feel whole

And you will look towards the guidance of others

But in these moments you must look within

For the lesson in healing always lies within.

O THE FOOL

A excerpt by the Phoenix Ra Tarot Deck Guidebook:
By Natasha Corbett

Key words: shenanigans, innocence, infinity, free spirit, risk, unexpected, folly, chaos, adventure.

Number 0 = Represents the great void, the cosmic abyss. Everything and nothing, no beginning and no end. Zero includes all other number frequencies and is associated with the source of creation. Infinity.

Astrological Ruler: Uranus – eccentric orbit which revolves around the sun on its side. Originality, independence. Creative uniqueness. Shakes things up, and disrupts the status quo. Rebellion against established authority.

Element: Air, the realm of ideas and inspiration before they are grounded in time and space. Air has a quickness to it. All things are possible and unlimited. Air is formless and ever-changing. **Path of Liberation**

UPRIGHT MEANING: The fool is a shapeshifter energy, one of divine madness, trickster, and wild card. The fool can cause havoc wherever it appears because they are not bound by the rules of society, they are rebelling without even realizing they are doing it. The fool says expect the unexpected. The fool has no home, it is a nomad, a wandering vagabond. Youth and eternal spring. The fool walks the fine line between inspiration and insanity. Fearless.

Both the beginning and end of the tarot cycle, some people chose to put the fool at the end. I personally like to see it as the start of the journey. The fool is the archetypical joker, and its presence survives in ordinary playing cards to this day. The Fool in a reading can foretell the coming of spontaneity and entertainment, amusement. The fool is the blank slate on the start of the journey of life. The fool is full of exuberance and energy, stumbling forwards with blind optimism. The fool steps foot on the journey, blissfully unaware of the cliff, or the dog snapping at their heels. The fool can represent a new opportunity coming your way, but it could include some risk as well. In order to move forwards you will have to take a leap of faith. The unlimited potential of the universe awaits you on the other side. It may also represent the beginning of a pilgrimage towards self-knowledge and eventually enlightenment.

Advice from The Fool: Look before you leap.

'Tude at The Louvre

A Short Story by Ryan Hook

Leslie and Miranda's relationship was as stale as the Doritos in between Miranda's seat cushion. So, Leslie decided to spend her Air Miles on a trip to Paris for the two of them. She expected a week of wine, cheese, and romance - she definitely had the former. When they arrived, the first few days were spent like any - getting over their jet lag, or for Miranda, getting over a first-class hangover.

It was just over halfway through their trip when they decided to check out the Louvre. On the taxi ride over, Leslie took in the French architecture while Miranda drank a 5-euro Chardonnay. The Louvre was as charming as ever and on the way over Leslie was able to talk to the taxi driver in french. For Leslie, today was going to be perfect.

As they both stepped out of the taxi, they looked at each other. Suddenly, Miranda's floppy visor, neon fanny pack, and subtle stars and stripe shirt became so obvious to Leslie she burst out laughing. Miranda looked confused then checked herself in the taxi window as it drove off and burst out laughing too. The two chuckled then sighed. Miranda brought out her water bottle of wine, spat the hair out from her mouth, and took a swig. When they approached the entrance, the security guard patted Leslie down, Miranda's eyes glazed over looking at Leslie with her grandma's crochet near her heart in her brown corduroy overalls. Leslie just looked around the Louvre, mouth gaping as wide as her blue eyes. Next, the security guard patted down Miranda. Miranda kind-of squirmed and sucked in her stomach. The security guard looked at the water bottle full of wine and asked to smell it.

Miranda said "n'es pas." Leslie applauded Miranda's french efforts in a quiet golf clap. Meanwhile, Miranda tried her best to remember how to say she had a medical condition in french.

The security guard grabbed it, unscrewed it halfway, until Miranda stole it back and downed the whole bottle of chardonnay. To the bystanders in the back, it probably looked like Miranada was a little dehydrated, to the people next to Miranda it looked like she confused the Louvre for a dive bar. By the time Miranda finished Leslie just walked in and headed for the paintings. That irritated Miranda, Leslie not standing by her.

Leslie admired every single cement tile and every brush stroke for the next two hours. Miranda got bored, so she decided to have a little fun. Miranda stood in line with Leslie to see the Mona Lisa, Leslie's fav. Miranda asked someone to take a picture of them, which was special to Leslie.

The man said "fromage," and just as he did, Miranda pulled down her cargo shorts and mooned the camera and crowd. Leslie's horror looked like an Edvard Munch painting and Miranada's ass looked like it hadn't seen the sun in centuries. Now it had seen about 100 strangers.

Miranda grabbed the phone, laughed, then showed Leslie.

Leslie did not laugh.

Unsurprised, the same security guard approached Miranda and asked them both to leave.

Leslie didn't speak to Miranda the whole way back to their hostel. There were only a few days left of the trip and the crowd was the only ass anyone was going to get. Miranda did what she did best: ignored the warning signs.

When they got home, a pandemic hit. The Canadian government urged international travellers to isolate two weeks due to Covid-19.

Along with the indigestion and heartburn, Miranda and Leslie were both shocked and relieved. They hadn't really talked to each other for the few days since getting back from the trip. Miranda tried to get over all the french cuisine by laying in bed with a bottle of Pepto-Bismol and the newest season of RuPaul's Drag Race, while Leslie hung out with her family trying to figure out what to do with her life. They figured if they isolated for two weeks it wouldn't change much anyways, and "for safety," they did. Miranda was getting sick of the way Leslie lost her breath when she ate anyways, so to her, this would be a nice reprieve.

It only took two days until Miranda got horny, bored, and lonely. Like anyone else in isolation, she got drunk. Then she booty-texted Leslie, "Hey, babe. Can't sleep. Can't seem to get me off - I mean, get you off my mind."

Leslie texted back, "I've missed you."

Miranda went silent and contemplated ghosting. Miranda wanted dirty talk. She didn't want feelings. She never wanted feelings.

The ellipsis from Leslie's conversation changed to another response, "Have you heard of Amazon Prime's streaming and delivery service? Watching your favourite shows and ordering your favourite shampoos and soaps has never been easier."

Leslie was no Casanova, but this was still weird.

Miranda broke up the awkward and said, "How else do you think I watch RuPaul, bitch?" Miranda stuffed her mouth with Cheetos and used her bed as a napkin until Leslie's next response.

Leslie replied, "Of course. And if you're looking for a new show, binging has never been easier with Netflix's newest series *Love is Blind*."

Miranda was surprised Leslie could even fathom mentioning a reality show. "I have both of those, weirdo, and I've been eating that show up like the Doritos in my seat cushions," Miranda said.

Leslie didn't reply for a couple minutes.

"If you like that. You know what you should really go for?" Leslie asked.

Miranda, being a horny bitch in the times she's not being a ruthless cunt, imagined Leslie in her bike shorts in Paris and segued the conversation with a simple, "I've got some rather dirty ideas."

And to Miranda's surprise, Leslie said, "While Wish.com's newest strap-on is both functional, it's also fashionable with a variety of new colours available."

"Wow -" Miranda actually got a bit wet. Where was this gal in Paris? "Babe, tell me how many colours." Miranda slid her sweatpants down.

"12," Leslie said.

"Oh, yeah? and what colours?" Miranda started to pant and breathe heavy.

"Red."

"Yeah?"

"Blue."

"Shut up."

"Green."

"Oh, God." Miranda was almost there.

"Yellow."

"What's gotten into you, babe? Oh my God."

"And magenta."

Miranda's leg shook as her eyes and the credits to *Love is Blind* rolled by.

She loosened her grip from her blankets and got light-headed as she sat up. Miranda grabbed her phone and texted, "Night, babe," then passed out.

Leslie said, "For a fast sleep, subscribe to *Gentle Whispering ASMR* on YouTube."

The next day, Miranda woke and her bedsheets looked like a crime scene sponsored by Cheetos and Lubraderm. She took her sheets off and threw them in the washing machine.

Paranoid of the scratch in her throat being Covid-19, she chugged a glass of water, grabbed a thermometer, and waited to be safe for another day. The days had started to become too similar, she thought. It'd been four days and each day she'd do the same thing: have her cat walk around her while she stretched out on the floor. She'd then make beans on toast and watch the news. It was a simple life, Miranda thought, which reminded her to watch *The Simple Life*.

While Leslie and Miranda went to Paris together in the hopes of setting their relationship straight, or *more gay*, but what came from it was two wildly different ideas of vacationing with two wildly different types of people.

Leslie wanted baguettes, and Miranda wanted burgers; Leslie wanted poetry, and Miranda wanted punk shows; Leslie wanted to take a gentle walk through *Pere LaChaise*, but all Miranda wanted to do was smash a bottle of wine over Jim Morrisson's grave and snort coke off Oscar Wilde's cobblestone.

So why were they together?

Basically, Miranda and Leslie were the single friends. After a few years, their mutual friends thought it'd be a good idea to set 'em up. For some reason, straight people think that because two friends are gay they should date, or at the very least, they should fuck. At that point, Miranda

was so single she mistook a picture of someone's armpit as Portia de Rossi's ass and Leslie had been on a sexual dry spell so long even her king-sized body pillow had moved on.

So, on their friend's recommendation, they went on a few dates. And after a year of at least getting something, albeit not much, they took their chances in Paris together. Miranda and Leslie withstood each other, though both sides had their grievances they'd never air. *You can't catch fruit flies with honesty.*

125

Miranda thought Leslie wasn't good enough in bed, and Leslie thought Miranda was too loud in bed. Leslie thought Miranda could "be nicer," while Miranda thought Leslie had no sense of humour. Call it lonely love, call it desperation, call it convenience, whatever it was they were in, it'd be hard to see them getting past the incident at the Louvre.

While Miranda ate her beans and toast, she laid plans for her social media wars and animal crossing with Paris Hilton and Nicole Richie singing "sanasa" in the background.

Legs crossed around her pillow, Miranda felt compelled to text Leslie, but she beat her to the punch. "For 29.99 you could be in one of these -" The screenshot below the message was a beautiful red lace top with black trim and a bustier, "- I'll even cover GST and Shipping."

Miranda was a bit confused, had Leslie just forgiven her?

Miranda said, "I don't know what's gotten into you, but I'll get one right now." Even though Miranda had lost her job, blown through her savings in Paris, and was waiting for her CERB payment, she figured $29.99 was a fine price to pay to get her this hot, "Ok. I ordered."

"Within 1-2 business days, your gift will arrive. In the meantime, Fiona Apple has a recent album out. Why not listen on Spotify?" Leslie linked Miranda to the album.

"Babe, Wow!" Fiona Apple really made Miranda wet but on her face. Leslie remembered that from their first date. Miranda went to her room, turned off the lights, and lit a candle and cigarette.

As the last song and Belmont came to an end, Miranda felt a bit guilty. Leslie actually seemed into her now.

While Leslie was a lot - always speaking french to everyone, wanting an "authentic" Parisian experience, and making friends with strangers - Miranda thought that perhaps even she was a lot. So she texted Leslie a simple, "Hey, babe, how was your day?"

Leslie replied instantly, "Fantastic. The new Peloton stationary bike has been really hitting my quads these days. Have you ever thought about getting one?"

What once was bright was surely dead. Miranda had already been feeling weight-conscious, so Leslie suggesting an exercise bike did not bode well.

"Hey, Leslie, why don't you take that Peloton bike and shove it up your ass. I'm sure shitting it out will sure be a workout," she said.

Miranda was upset and didn't bother to look back for Leslie's response. She threw her phone and turned to her two vibrators she nicknamed "Pel" and "Tom" for a real stationary ride. She fell asleep not long after.

Miranda, despite her own workout, still woke up looking like Gordon Ramsey's lost child. She threw her sheets in the washing machine. Miranda knew she blew up too fast on Leslie, and that wasn't fair. She probably just actually loved her Peloton bike. Full of surprises, she thought.

Miranda grabbed her phone within her bedroom Machu Picchu and saw there was a text already from Leslie.

The text said, "You're right. I'm sorry. I don't even like Peloton bikes. I just wanted to impress you. Perhaps you'd enjoy a Bowflex?"

Miranda burst out cry-laughing, "Damn, bitch, you got me," Leslie must have been kidding, she thought.

"I'm sorry I overreacted. I've just been a bit self conscious this week. You know, I really should start working out. How much is a Peloton?"

"2,905.00. I'll even cover the GST and shipping."

"Wow, thanks, babe."

"You're welcome. Speaking of sarcasm, Tom Segura has a new comedy special out."

"You read my mind, babe, I was going to watch that today after lunch. I'm gonna hop in the shower. Ttyl."

Miranda hopped in the shower and as she scrubbed her back an old Dorito Cool Ranch chip fell off and dissolved into the bathtub. Miranda didn't even notice. She couldn't stop thinking about how sexy Leslie would actually look on a Peloton bike with little beads of sweat dripping off her belly button. She thought of herself barging in and ripping off Leslie's tight bicycle shorts. The bathroom started to get steamy with Miranda's fantasy. The birds beside her bathroom window fluttered away as she moaned. Miranda stopped the shower and put her pajamas back on.

A few more days went by and it dawned on Miranda how much she actually loved Leslie. Before this, her internet bookmarks were stills of Portia de Rossi in a bikini. Now, Miranda was cruising Leslie's socials for duck-lip pictures and selfies. Not only that, but Leslie was making Miranda look and feel better too. Since isolation, Miranda had started working out. She'd bought a bidet, started taking vitamins, invested into cryptocurrency, and added a whole new wardrobe to her closet, all thanks to Leslie. And even though Miranda was burning through money as fast as a downtown drunk goes through a bottle of Russian Prince, she thought that maybe Leslie was leading to something.

They only had one more night until they could see each other and so far they'd been safe from getting sick. The only time Miranda felt sick was puking up the new Vitamin Supplements Leslie recommended after a night of eating pizza in bed. Miranda texted her that night "I'm scared" while she finished *The Walking Dead*.

"You didn't enjoy the newest season of The Walking Dead? Have you tried AMC's other hit, Sons of Anar-"

"No. It's not the show. It's that I've fallen more in love with you. And I can't even believe you can forgive me for what happened at the Louvre."

"The Louvre, or the Louvre Museum, is the world's largest art museum and a historic monument in Paris, France. A central landmark of the city, it is located on the Right Bank of the Seine in the city's first arrondissement."

"Ok. Yes. I know you remember. You don't have to rub it in. I just feel bad. I never apologized, and if you know me, you know that I don't apologize." Miranda swallowed her pride, along with a shot of tequila, and finally said it: "I'm sorry."

Leslie didn't answer that night. And they both woke up the next day free to go outside.

Miranda felt free, but she felt the weight of guilt for treating Leslie so horribly on their trip. Usually she would have said "fuck Leslie." She would have made up a bunch of rumours about

her to her friends and Leslie's and then blamed her friends for setting her up with that stuck-up bitch.

But the two weeks away had changed Miranda. This Leslie she got to know changed Miranda. She finally became someone who could admit they were wrong. As Miranda took a walk and looked at the Edmonton skyline, she realized how much she had really missed everything, including Leslie. Miranda resolved to be patient.

The next day Leslie texted Miranda, "I need to see you, Miranda. Let's go for a walk at my favourite spot. I got you a mask, gloves, and hand sanitizer too."

Miranda was excited albeit a bit nervous. Was Leslie going to pop the big question? Was she busy getting a ring? Is that why she didn't answer? Maybe there'll be a ring on the gloves she gives me, she hoped. Miranda couldn't remember Leslie's favourite spot so she messaged the friend that set them up and she said to go to *The End of the World*.

Miranda texted, "Oh, of course. How could I forget?"

When Miranda got there she walked to the dirt path leading to *The End of the World* and saw a note with a surgical mask and hand sanitizer in a plastic bag: *For Miranda*. This was so romantic, in a Mad Max sort of way.

Miranda walked down the dirt path and saw Leslie by the edge of the steep drop off at The End of the World. *The End of the World* was the skeleton of a former house that fell into the North Saskatchewan River; now, it's a place where underrage kids drink and smoke weed. In the distance, the sun was setting while it reflected off the fast flow of the River, the clouds were dancing pink with the painted blue sky. It was spring but it felt like an autumn day. The sun was beating down on Leslie's unflattering navy blue University sweater, and Miranda thought the blue of her surgical mask really brought out Leslie's eyes. Miranda felt ashamed but couldn't stop looking at Leslie's glow. She approached her somewhat frantic: "Look, I know that I've been -"

"What a gorgeous day." Leslie stared out towards the North Saskatchewan River.

Miranda was confused but played it cool - nodding her head and putting her hands in her pockets, "Pfft yeah, like, totally."

"Look, my time in isolation had me thinking..." Leslie said.

"Uh-huh."

Leslie paused and took a deep breath. Miranda had "yes" on the tip of her lips waiting for Leslie to propose.

"For the first few days of isolation, I was so stagnant, willing to accept what this was -" Leslie gestured between the 2 meters of space between them, "- but after a week and a half of no social media, no texting, no email, no Skype, and finally getting to the end of the paperwork to get my online identity back, I feel alive again. I feel like I understand myself better too."

"Wait, what?"

"I know, Right?! It took me literally losing my identity to find the real me

130

again. Irony." "Wait, what?"

"And I finally know what I need, Miranda."

"Wait. Hold on! So you haven't been texting me for the past week and a half?"

"Yeah - I mean, no. Sorry I wasn't replying. I accidentally opened an email from some Pakistani hacker. They almost drained my bank account. Tried to convince my Mom to buy a Peloton. Luckily I'm getting all the money back. I had to spend all of yesterday figuring it out."

"Bank account's clear, hey?" Miranda thought about the Ikea Catologue of worthless shit she paid for because of those fuckin' Packistani hackers. She knew she shouldn't have had to WD-40 a Peloton before using it. No wonder her vitamins made her sick. And she'd only been getting chubbier from her meal replacement.

None of that shit actually did anything.

"Anyways, I've realized that what happened at the Louvre, it's just not something I can forgive, and knowing you, you won't apologize. I know you well enough, and I finally know myself better enough to know we can't be together."

Miranda looked out onto the Edmonton River Valley. With the steep edge and sunset surrounding them both, she looked around, took a deep breath, and realized that regardless of the future, Leslie still changed her.

"You know, it really is beautiful, Leslie," Miranda said.

Leslie went into her bag and opened Miranda's favourite bag of chips: Cool Ranch Doritos.

Leslie's cheek bones raised indicating a smile from behind her surgical mask. Miranda and Leslie enjoyed their last moments together, safe from illness and blessed to watch a sunset.

Leslie looked at Miranda's hands, "Oh, I forgot to give you your gloves." Leslie went into her backpack with her gloves on and gave a pair to Miranda. Miranda looked at the ring finger on the left hand glove, empty.

"You know what, I actually have something for you too, Leslie."

Miranda reached into her backpack and took out the magenta Strapon she bought from Wish.com, "Here, you got this for me."

Ryan Hook is a writer, musician, and spoken word poet.

His mission is to bring Sound and Story and he has worked as a music journalist for Vue Weekly, BeatRoute, and Exclaim! as well as being a published short story writer. When he's not writing he is a songwriter and recording artist for his band, Baby Boy and the Earthly Delights. Whether it's writing, music, or travelling, he bides by the philosophy that life is a playground and nothing is off limits.

Upon Returning
A Poem by Layla

The secret that no one tells you,

about returning to your body after being dissociated from it for so long,

is that once you are finally home,

you realise that the mess you have made now needs to be tended to.

The scars you see from the time you were away seem undeserving.

The harm you have done to your vessel reveals a pain within yourself you were not aware you were hiding from. Nor certain you could handle.

The hardest part of coming home…

the part that no one tells you about,

how to forgive and move forward,

Upon Returning.

The Gallery

A photo by Elliott Haviland

FACUTY CLOSED
THIS FACILITY IS CLOSED
by mom

A photo by Elliott Haviland

a Vallen farces
dia
meats & seafood

A photo by Elliott Haviland

WHITEROCK

B RANCH NAS

CLOSED UNTIL FURTHER NOTICE

A photo by Elliott Haviland

CAPRISE

SHOWCASE THEATRES

FOR THE HEALTH & SAFETY OF OUR OWN GUEST & STAFF WE ARE

TEMPORARILY CLOSED THANKS FOR YOUR SUPPORT FOR UPDATES

VISIT HOLLYWOODCINEMA.CA

HOPE TO SEE YOU ALL AGAIN SOON

CTEKS MAPLE SUSHI

CAPERE

A photo by Elliott Haviland

LV
STAY IN YOUR CAR until you can keep
2 metres apart
2 m
2 m
Help keep parks open
metro vancouver REGIONAL PARKS

Sabina Brouwer

Sabina Brouwer

Sabina Brouwer

As a Christian painter, Covid was a time to slow down. To reflect. To be thankful for what we were missing. Family became more precious, health became more precious and friends and freedom became more precious. But it was also a time to invest in myself and with more time at home an opportunity to paint. In a sort of thankful way in itself, it helped me to calm the chaos and explore more of my talents.